Dream Catcher

Ryan Adkins

Archway Publishing books may be ordered through booksellers or by contacting:

Archway Publishing
1663 Liberty Drive
Bloomington, IN 47403
www.archwaypublishing.com
1-(888)-242-5904

Because of the dynamic nature of the Internet, any web addresses or links contained in this book may have changed since publication and may no longer be valid. The views expressed in this work are solely those of the author and do not necessarily reflect the views of the publisher, and the publisher hereby disclaims any responsibility for them.

Any people depicted in stock imagery provided by Thinkstock are models, and such images are being used for illustrative purposes only.

Certain stock imagery © Thinkstock.

ISBN: 978-1-4808-0326-8 (sc)
ISBN: 978-1-4808-0328-2 (hc)
ISBN: 978-1-4808-0327-5 (e)

Printed in the United States of America

Archway Publishing rev. date: 10/16/13

It was the first day of school for Dorian Hubble,
And making new friends was so much *trouble.*

Was it because of his wild *imagination* —
Dreaming of rockets, Martians, and outer space stations?

The other kids laughed, giggled, and grinned,
Making it difficult for him to fit in.

Later that night, lying lonely in bed,

In came his mother, who lovingly said,

"You can do anything you set your mind to,

And with this dream catcher, your *dreams* will come true!"

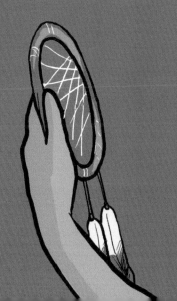

And with that dream catcher, Dorian wished for a friend

And wished that his loneliness would come to an end.

But little did he know that it would reply

By sending a *star* from the deep and dark sky.

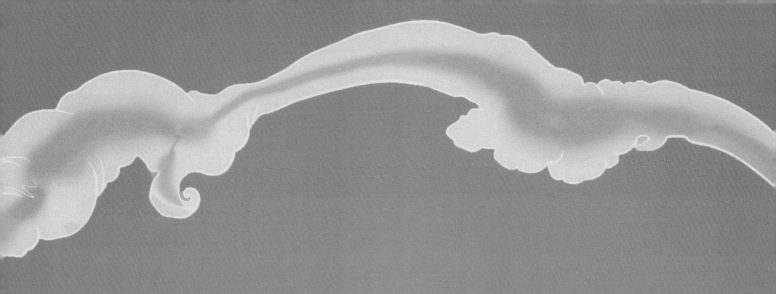

With a red jester hat and skin white as snow,

The star did not speak, not even "Hello."

From where the star came, he did not know,

But from where the star came, *Dorian* wanted to go.

"Take me far, far away!" Dorian wished.
So the shooting-star creature granted just this.

And before he could even count to two,
Into the dream catcher Dorian *flew!*

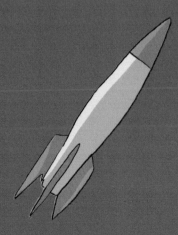

He flew through a tunnel that twisted like rope,
Which sparkled with colors like a kaleidoscope.

At the end of the tunnel was a *magical* place
Where even the wildest of dreams could be chased.

The land teemed with *creatures* both big and small.
There were far too many to count them all:

Cloud orcas, Cheshires, and fluttering flower-flies.
You wouldn't believe them even with your own eyes!

So filled with wonder, joy, and glee.

So little time yet so much to see.

Though he wished to stay longer and continue to *play,*

Dorian realized he had school the next day!

So back through the dream catcher Dorian went,
Never to forget the time he there spent.

Now once again lying lonely in bed,
With a smile on his face he *joyfully* said,

"Dare to be *different,* for no one can match it!
Keep chasing your dream, for someday you'll catch it!"

About the Author

Ryan Adkins earned a bachelor's degree in literature, media, and communications from the Georgia Institute of Technology. He is the founder and president of iLLUSIONÀGE PRODUCTIONS, specializing in graphic art and design. Ryan resides in Atlanta, Georgia, where he continues to pursue a career in the animation industry.

CPSIA information can be obtained
at www.ICGtesting.com
Printed in the USA
LVIC04n1323011113

359512LV00002B/5